# The King Who
# Banned the Dark

For my family

First published in the UK in 2018 by
Pavilion Books Company Limited
43 Great Ormond Street
London
WC1N 3HZ

Publisher and Editor: Neil Dunnicliffe
Assistant Editor: Harriet Grylls
Designer: Lee-May Lim

ISBN: 9781843653974

A CIP catalogue record for this book is available from the British Library.

10 9 8 7 6 5 4

Reproduction by Mission Production Ltd., Hong Kong
Printed by GPS Group, Slovenia

This book can be ordered directly from the publisher
online at www.pavilionbooks.com, or try your local bookshop.

# The King Who Banned the Dark

PAVILION

There was once a little boy who
was afraid of the dark.

There's nothing so unusual about that.

Most children are afraid of the dark at one time or another.

and he decided that when
he became King,

But this little boy
was a Prince,

he would do something about the dark.

He would **ban** it.

On the first morning of his reign, the King told his advisors about his plan.

And so, the advisors started to spread rumours about the dark.

The people had never really worried about the dark before,
but all of a sudden it started to seem like a really bad thing.

So they marched to the Palace and demanded a ban on the dark.

said the King.

And because everyone had got what they thought they wanted,
everyone thought they were happy.

Even when the real sun set, the artificial sun kept shining. All day and all night it glowed in the sky.

Curtains were taken down. Anti-dark hats were issued. Lamps shone from every window twenty-four hours a day, seven days a week.

The people stayed up all night celebrating, which was easy, because it never got dark.

But soon the people were tired of celebrating. In fact they were just **tired**. With the lights on all the time, no one could sleep at all, and with no real night time, the days dragged on forever.

The people had made a mistake. They realised pretty quickly that they needed the dark back.

But if anyone tried to switch their lights off, the Light Inspectors would make them pay a fine.

As the King tried to sleep under the glare
of a hundred lightbulbs, he
heard shouts from outside the Palace.

To get the people excited about the Dark Ban again, the advisors decided to throw a big party.

But the people weren't as silly as the King's advisors
thought they were.

Whisper by whisper, they hatched their own plan.

On the night of the great celebration,
the King stood on the roof to watch the fireworks.

But the sky was so bright
that when the first firework went off
nothing could be seen at all.

The King sighed.

Meanwhile, elsewhere in the Kingdom, a house switched off its lights.
The Light Inspectors knocked on the door.

At that moment, the lights in the house next door went off.

And the lights in the house next to that.  And the house next to that.

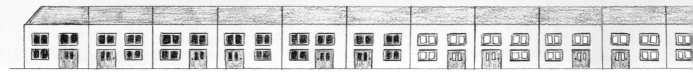

The same thing was happening on the street next to that,

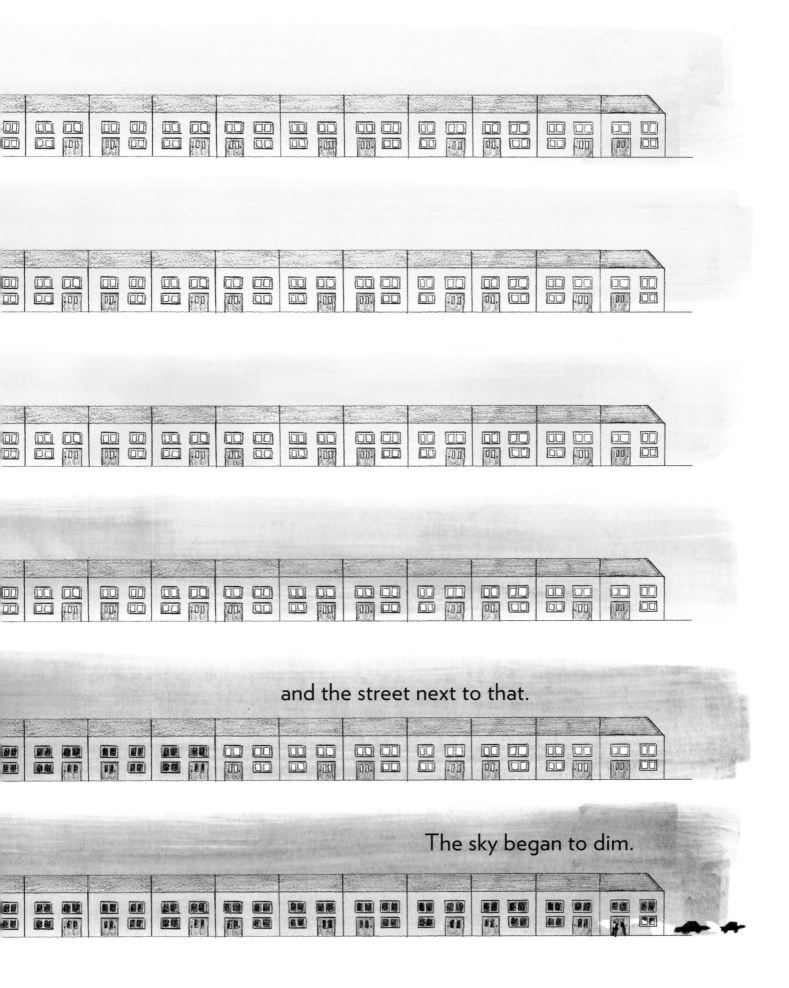

and the street next to that.

The sky began to dim.

The Light Inspectors began to panic and called for back-up.

All the guards at the Palace rushed to help them.

And that's when, with the Palace unguarded, a small group of people climbed up the walls and switched off the very last switch.

The sky went dark. The King shuddered.

"We must turn the sun back on, Your Majesty!"
shouted the advisors. "We must crush the
uprising! We must punish the people!"

"Shush," said the King. "Look!"

The lights had gone out just in time
for the grand finale.

Instead of punishing anyone, the King lifted the ban on the dark.

And now, every year on the same night, the people set off fireworks in the darkness – to remind themselves of what they almost lost.

The King is still sometimes a little bit scared of the dark,
but he sleeps with a night light these days.

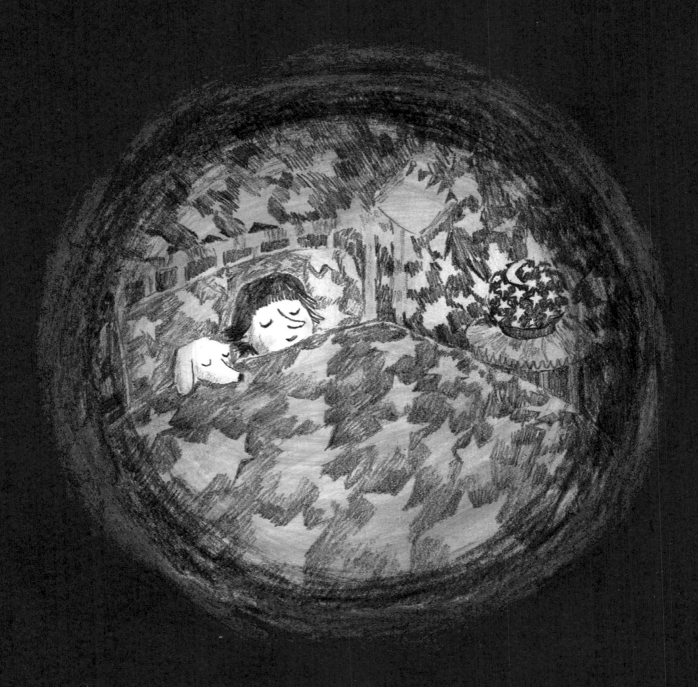

If only he'd done that in the first place,
this whole mess could have been avoided.